BEING DAN

THERE ARE ALWAYS TWO SIDES
TO EVERY STORY.

TITLES IN TWO SIDES:

GIRL NEXT DOOR
Karen Moncrieffe

SAM
Emma Norry

YOU DON'T CARE
Luisa Plaja

STOP
Jenni Spangler

LOOKING AFTER MUM
Roy Apps

BRUISED
Donna David

HOME
Karen Moncrieffe

BREATHE
Karen Moncrieffe

UNITED
Emma Norry

TORN
Jenni Spangler

BEING DAN
Donna David

CHANGE
Chitra Soundar

Badger Publishing Limited, Oldmedow Road, Hardwick Industrial Estate,
King's Lynn PE30 4JJ

Telephone: 01438 791037

www.badgerlearning.co.uk

BEING DAN

DONNA DAVID

Being Dan ISBN 978-1-78837-391-3

Publisher/Senior Editor: Danny Pearson
Editor: Claire Morgan
Copyeditor: Cheryl Lanyon
Designer: Bigtop Design Ltd
Cover Illustration: Dave Robbins

4 6 8 10 9 7 5 3

CHAPTER 1
PASSPORT

Dan threw his school shirt on the back of his chair and took off his sports bra. He looked at himself in the mirror. He sucked in his stomach, turned one way and then the other. Then, with a sigh of relief, he let it out again. Dan smiled.

“Hang on,” Dan called as someone knocked on his bedroom door. He grabbed his hoodie off the end of the bed and quickly pulled it on. “Come in.”

His mum pushed open his door and leant against the door frame looking in.

"You OK?" Dan asked after a few moments' silence.

His mum held up an envelope in her hand and waved it back and forth. "It's here," she said.

Dan took two quick steps across the room and snatched the envelope out of her hand. His heart raced as he tore it open and the passport fell to the floor. He quickly picked it up and clutched it against his chest.

"Well," said Mum, "are you going to look? Or shall I?"

Dan pulled the passport away from his body and tapped it against the palm of his free hand. "No," he said. "I will."

Dan sat down on his bed. His mum walked into the room and took a seat next to him. She put her arm around his shoulder and squeezed gently. Dan took a deep breath and opened the passport. He flicked through to the personal details page and stopped. He looked down at his familiar face.

His floppy dark hair had been brushed to the side for the photo. Dan's usual style of hair over his eyes wasn't acceptable for the Passport Office.

But Dan wasn't interested in the photo. His eyes quickly scanned the text and he smiled when he saw it.

Daniel Morris.

It was his name. They'd changed it. And, more importantly, under 'sex' was the letter M. M for male.

Dan looked at his mum. Her eyes were watery but she blinked quickly and the tears disappeared.

"They changed it," said Dan. After all this time, he'd finally got it.

Mum pulled him in close and kissed the top of his head. "They changed it," she echoed.

"What's going on?" came a voice from the landing. Lucy had walked out of her bedroom and was looking into Dan's room. "What have you got there?" Lucy stepped into the room and took the passport out of Dan's hands before he had time to speak.

"My passport," he said.

"I can see that," said Lucy, already flicking through the pages to get to the photograph page.

"They changed my name," said Dan.

"I can see that too, Sophie," said Lucy.

"Lucy!" Mum said with a stern tone.

Dan flinched at the use of the name Sophie, the name he'd been given when he'd been assigned female at birth.

"My name's Dan," he said. His voice was almost a whisper.

Without another word, Lucy threw the passport on the bed and stormed across Dan's bedroom.

As she marched out of the room she slammed the door shut causing Mum and Dan to flinch. They sat still as they listened to her bang downstairs and turn the TV up loud in the kitchen.

"Just what's her problem?" asked Dan, throwing himself down on the bed.

Mum sighed sadly. "She's worried," she said. "About you and about starting university. Moving away is a big deal for her. She'll come around. You just need to give her some more time."

"She's had time," snapped Dan. "I've had counselling for years. You've had counselling for years. I'm seeing specialist doctors; doctors who support me and help me and who know what they're talking about. And she still thinks it's a phase, doesn't she?"

Mum avoided Dan's eyes.

"Doesn't she?" said Dan again, this time a little more quietly.

"Yes."

"It's not," said Dan. "She's wrong."

"I know," said Mum, taking Dan's hand in her own. "I know and so does Lucy. She just hasn't come to terms with it yet."

CHAPTER 2
BLOCKERS

Lucy

Lucy was finding dinner kind of awkward. Mum was talking in her too-bright voice. Dad occasionally answered Mum's questions, but soon even he tired of her story about the next-door-neighbour's cat.

In the end, Lucy just couldn't bear it.

"Why are we all just pretending that everything's OK?" she asked. "Why do you all think that having a life-changing operation is not a big deal?"

Mum tried to reach for Lucy's hand but Lucy pulled away.

"And what about the risks? The consequences?" Lucy asked. She threw her cutlery onto her plate.

"We know all about the risks," said Dad. "This isn't an overnight decision. We've been asking questions of the experts for a very long time now."

A look of defiance flashed in Dan's eyes. "You'd know all of this if you just spoke to me about it, Lucy. You'd know that it's the first thing I think of when I wake up in the morning and the last thing I think of at night."

Lucy took a deep breath. "I just don't get why I'm the only one who can see the problem here. When I was 12, I wanted Ryan's name tattooed on my wrist. Imagine if you'd let me do that!"

"It's hardly the same, love," said Dad. He looked tired. He rubbed his hand across his face. "If you'd come to the counselling sessions then you'd..."

"Then I'd what?" snapped Lucy. "Be brainwashed into thinking that it was OK to give a 14-year-old hormone blockers? Be forced to think that it was

OK to let a 14-year-old make a decision about transitioning? Has anyone stopped to think that she might change her mind?"

"It's 'he'," interrupted Dad, sharply.

"And I won't change my mind," snapped Dan. His voice was as loud as it could be before it became shouting.

Mum quickly put her hand on his arm. "Dan can come off the hormone blockers at any time. He's known that from day one. He can pause things or stop them completely whenever he wants to."

Dan grimaced at the thought.

"What sort of doctor lets a 14-year-old go on hormone blockers, though?" asked Lucy.

"Experts in their field," said Dan.

"But they don't know the full side effects," said Lucy.

"And that's why we didn't take the decision lightly, Lucy," said Dad. "We don't take any of these decisions lightly. We talk to every expert available to us. We know the risks."

"Do you want me to tell you the risks for trans children who aren't listened to?" asked Dan. "Do you want to know how many self-harm?"

"Dan," said Mum quietly. "We don't need to..."

"We do," said Dan sharply. "Shall I tell you how many trans kids attempt suicide? Or how many succeed?"

"I'm on your side," said Lucy quietly. "I get that it's tough. And it was OK when you were six. It was kind of cool when you picked clothes from the boys' section and you refused to play with my old toys." Lucy sighed. "But you're 14 now. Do you know how hard things are going to be if you carry on?"

"Yeah," said Dan standing up from the table. "Yeah I do. And do you have any idea how hard it will be if I don't?"

Dan walked away from the table. His shoulders drooped and his head hung low. "Thanks for dinner," he mumbled.

Lucy watched as he walked away. Mum and Dad were both back to picking at their dinner. The conversation was over.

CHAPTER 3
BIG SISTER

Dan lay on his bed and stared up at the ceiling. A knot of anger twisted in his stomach. Lucy had watched him grow up. She knew him better than anyone and yet she still couldn't accept him as he was.

To begin with, Lucy had been his biggest ally. Dan remembered having a huge tantrum when his parents tried to get him to wear a dress to his Aunty Jo's wedding. They'd begged him, bribed him and yelled at him. In the end, Lucy had stormed up to his room where she'd grabbed a smart shirt and pair of trousers. Then she'd thrown open Dad's drawer and pulled out a thin, red tie.

"Here," she'd said, marching back down the stairs. "Why can't she just wear this?"

Dan could not have loved his sister any more on that day. She was his hero who'd do anything for him.

Not anymore.

He'd been Dan at home for a few months before he transitioned outside of the home. His friends at school had been brilliant — when his name was changed on the school register and he'd stopped changing in the girls' changing room, they'd all been really cool with it. Some had asked questions and some still did. To begin with, a teacher or a friend would forget and they'd call him 'Sophie', but Dan hadn't minded too much. And that only happened in the beginning anyway.

Lucy seemed to be the only person who had a problem with it. She was the one person he'd expected to 'get' it. He'd always looked up to her; she was his big sister and she'd always looked out for him.

But not this time. This time she was refusing to listen. She wouldn't go to the family counselling sessions and she wouldn't even talk to Dan about what he was feeling.

Dan pulled several notepads from his bookshelf and sat down on his bed. They were his diaries. When Dan had first started seeing his counsellor four years ago, she'd asked him to try writing a diary. She said it might help him, and it had. It had helped him organise how he was feeling, and whenever he found something hard to talk about, he just wrote it down.

Dan flicked through his earliest entries, the ones he'd written when he was nearly 11. He frowned as he remembered how much he'd hated his school uniform back then. He'd devoted a whole page to moaning about the itchy cardigans with fiddly buttons. Not long after showing his mum that entry, she'd marched into school and asked them if there was any reason why he couldn't wear the boys' jumpers. There wasn't, and getting ready for school became a lot easier after that.

The entries that he'd written around a year later were the most difficult to read. His body had started to change around about then. He'd spent every waking moment of every day feeling uncomfortable in his own skin. The difference between how Dan looked and how he felt became wider and wider, until living in his own body was almost unbearable. Dan would stare in the mirror and hate what he saw. He'd look at his tiny, developing breasts and feel like he was drowning. That's when the self-harming started.

His mum and dad had become desperate. Desperate for help. Desperate for solutions.

So, after months of counselling, Dan had started on hormone blockers to stop these unwelcome signs of becoming a young woman. There was no exaggeration when Dan told his counsellor that the injections had saved his life.

Flicking through the pages, Dan was sure that a complete stranger would be able to pick out the month that the hormone blockers started. Angry, distressed scribblings were replaced with calmer and more hopeful entries. The hormone blockers didn't give Dan the body he wanted, but they gave him time. The treatment gave him time to breathe without the threat of puberty.

But that was two years ago now. According to Mum, Lucy needed more time. Dan needed less. The next stage in his treatment was hormone therapy and that was so far away. Dan wanted to start now. Today. He knew he had to wait but it just didn't seem fair. He'd known he was a boy from his very earliest memory. Surely that was long enough?

CHAPTER 4
BAD DAYS

Lucy

"I've finished," said Lucy and she stood up from the dinner table.

"Hang on," said Mum. "We need to talk."

"It's not me you need to talk to," snapped Lucy.

"Please," said Mum.

Lucy looked annoyed but she sat back down.

"Your mum and I have been talking," said Dad, "and you've got to stop this, Lucy. Dan's struggling. He's got to wait for his hormone therapy and he doesn't want to."

"You need to listen to him," said Mum. "Really listen."

Lucy gave a sharp laugh. "Listen? Every time I speak you guys interrupt me."

"Because you keep deadnaming him, Lucy. His name's Dan and you keep calling him Sophie. Do you know the damage that you could do?" Mum's hands trembled as she spoke.

Dad put his hand on Mum's shoulder. "Dan's got some big decisions to make, Lucy, and he needs our support. He needs a safe space to think and it needs to be here with us. With you."

Lucy traced her fingers around the swirls in the wooden kitchen table. She opened her mouth to speak but her voice cracked. Dad shuffled his chair closer and held her hand.

"What is it, love?"

"I miss her," said Lucy. "I miss Sophie," Lucy's shoulders began to shake with the effort of holding back her tears, “and I don’t understand how you don’t.”

“I did,” said Dad, pulling Lucy closer. “To begin with I missed Sophie all the time. I was so used to my three girls. I was in the minority but I liked it. Kept me on my toes!”

Lucy smiled through her tears.

“But then I realised,” said Dad, “that I never really had two daughters. I only ever had one: a kind, fierce, intelligent and amazing daughter. And I had a son. I’d always had a son. It just took me a while to realise it.”

“And his personality hasn’t changed,” said Mum. “He’s still the little kid you grew up with. The one who followed you everywhere, who absolutely adored you, who never wanted anyone else to change his nappy or feed him his dinner.”

“You’ve got a brother, Lucy,” said Dad gently. “I know that’s not what we told you when he was born, but he's telling us now. You've got a caring, funny, brave and scared brother. And he needs you. He's always needed you and he does now more than ever."

Lucy sobbed loudly as she leant into her dad, not trying to stop her tears. Her nose streamed and Mum handed her a tissue.

"But… it's… all… so… quick," she stuttered between big, gulping breaths.

"Is it?" asked Mum gently. "How old do you think Dan was when he first told us that he was a boy? That the hospital had made a mistake?"

Lucy shrugged.

"He was four," said Mum. "He was told to sit with the girls at nursery and he came out that afternoon and told me that his teacher had got it wrong. His teacher had put him with the girls and she'd got it all wrong."

Lucy tried to remember. She tried to remember her four-year-old sister telling her that she was really a boy. But she couldn't and surely you wouldn't forget a conversation like that?

"She never told me," said Lucy. "I was with her all the time and she never once told me until she started secondary school."

"You guys did everything together," said Dad.

"Exactly," said Lucy.

Dad paused. "So he didn't need to tell you, Lucy. He thought you knew."

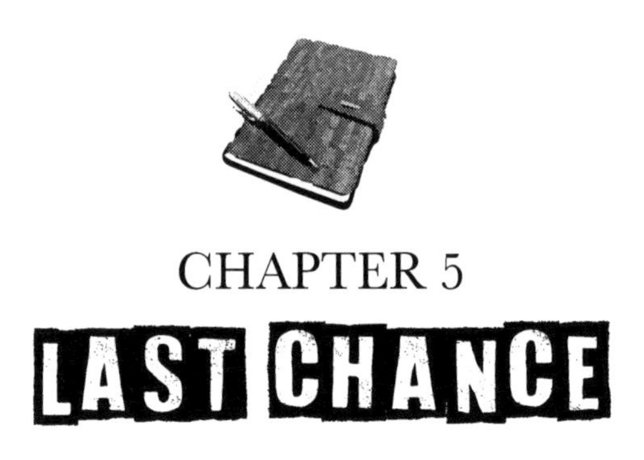

CHAPTER 5
LAST CHANCE

Perhaps it will be easier once Lucy leaves for university, thought Dan. If he didn't have to see her every day, then maybe he could forget what she thought. Maybe he'd stop caring.

Or maybe not.

Whenever Dan tried to talk to Lucy, it was like he couldn't find the right words or he couldn't find the right answers, and it would just end up in an argument. Now he didn't even bother trying.

Dan looked at his diaries. It was so much easier to write things down. It was reassuring to know that you could cross things out or never have to show what you'd written. You didn't have to look at someone's reaction and imagine what they were thinking while they read your deepest secrets and hopes.

Dan picked up a pencil and tore a sheet of paper out of his notepad. He chewed his pencil thoughtfully and then started to write.

Dear Lucy,

It probably seems like I've spent the last couple of years disagreeing with everything you say. But I want you to know that I really have been trying to see it from your point of view. I've talked to the other guys at my support group — some of them are trans and some of them are friends or family of trans teenagers — and they've helped me understand a little bit what it's like for you.

They told me that most people our age don't really think about their gender because it just feels 'right' to them. Like, why would you worry about what it means to be a girl when you just ARE a girl?

But for me, I've thought about it every day for as long as I can remember. I feel like there was some big mistake when I was born and I ended up in the wrong body. Some days I want to scream and shout that it isn't fair. It's not fair that nature got it so wrong. It's not fair that I have to wait for hormone therapy. It's not fair that the doctors say I'm too young to start now, today, this minute. Sometimes this makes me so angry that I feel like hurting myself.

At the same time, I know how lucky I am. Jimmy, the man who runs the support group, said that when he was younger and told everyone that he was male, no one understood. There was nowhere for him to go, no one for him to talk to, no treatments available. Listening to Jimmy makes me realise how lucky I really am. Then I feel guilty.

Some days it's just too much. I need a quiet space, somewhere safe. I want that place to be here, with you and Mum and Dad.

I would love you to come to counselling with us. They'll be able to answer so many of your questions and you can ask me as well. I'm not scared of the questions. It's much worse when you don't ask any.

Love Dan

Dan carefully folded the letter in half and put it on top of his diaries. He pushed his sleeves up and looked at the fading marks on his arms; the marks he'd hidden from Lucy for so long. Mum and Dad knew how bad things had got, but Lucy didn't. What if Lucy read his diaries and still didn't support him? Dan's stomach turned at the thought.

But Lucy was his sister. She'd always looked out for him in the past. She'd always protected him. Dan had to trust that she would do the same again.

She was leaving for university tomorrow. This was their last chance.

CHAPTER 6
RAINBOW FLAG

“You look tired,” said Mum as Lucy walked into the kitchen. Her hair was sticking up where she’d slept on it and yesterday’s mascara was smudged down her face.

“Didn’t sleep much,” mumbled Lucy as she sat down at the kitchen table.

“Nerves?” asked Mum.

“Yeah, must have been,” said Lucy, but she was looking out of the kitchen door towards the stairs. “Is anyone else awake yet?”

"Your dad's gone to get petrol and Dan's already been down for breakfast. He must be getting dressed now."

"He's coming then?" asked Lucy.

"You're leaving for uni," said Mum, resting her arm on Lucy's shoulder. "Of course he's coming to drop you off. We have every intention of crying on your doorstep and embarrassing you in front of your new friends."

*

The journey to Manchester took just over an hour. As Dad drove, Mum fired off a few questions about when Lucy's first lectures were and which modules she thought she might take. Lucy answered automatically but she wasn't really paying attention. She was watching Dan.

Dan hadn't spoken to Lucy all morning. When Lucy had gone to bed late last night, she'd found a pile of diaries on her bed and a letter from Dan. She'd read them. And then she'd reread them.

Her eyes were sore from crying and her head ached from lack of sleep.

She'd tried to talk to Dan this morning but Dad had kept yelling at them all to hurry up. Lucy had been in and out to the car with her clothes and books and a million different kitchen utensils that Mum had insisted were essential for student living.

Dan was staring out of the window. His hair was covering his eyes and he was biting the skin on the edge of his thumbnail. He was wearing his everyday uniform of blue jeans and a hoodie. He caught Lucy's eye and Lucy tried to smile, but Dan turned away quickly. Lucy put out her hand to touch him on the shoulder but she let it drop back down to the seat. He was too far away.

*

The Fresher's Fayre was in the sports hall and it was heaving with new students. There were rows and rows of stands showing the best clubs that Manchester University had to offer. Mum and

Dad had gone to get some lunch and Lucy was pleased when Dan said he'd wander over with her to have a look.

Lucy still wanted to talk to Dan. She needed to. But this wasn't the right place. It was too noisy. There were too many people about.

"Let's just look at every stand and then we'll find somewhere quieter," said Lucy, turning to Dan, but there was no one there. One moment he'd been right behind her, waiting to follow, and the next he was gone.

People were bumping into Lucy as they tried to make their way past her. She pulled out her phone to ring Dan, but just as she unlocked the screen, something caught her eye.

The brightly coloured flag was a few tables away. It stood taller than the other stands in the hall, so you'd be able to see it if you looked up from anywhere in the hall. It was the rainbow flag of the Manchester University LGBT Society and straightaway Lucy knew where Dan would be.

Lucy pushed her way through the crowd until she spotted him. He was talking to an older student at the stand. Dan was holding a few leaflets in his hand and he was smiling. A big, wide smile. Lucy felt an aching in her chest — it had been such a long time since she'd seen that smile.

Slowly, Lucy made her way towards them both. Dan was waving his arms and talking quickly. He looked excited.

Dan stopped mid-sentence as Lucy walked towards him.

"Hi," said the older student. "My name's Jake. I'm a committee member for the LGBT Society here." He handed Lucy a leaflet. "Are you interested in joining?"

Lucy looked at Dan who was staring at the leaflets in his hand, refusing to make eye contact.

"Yeah," said Lucy. "Yeah I am."

Dan looked up quickly. He frowned in confusion. "You are?"

Lucy nodded.

"Do you guys know each other?" asked Jake.

"Yeah," said Lucy. She smiled nervously. "This is my brother... Dan."

Jake smiled and moved away to talk to another student.

"I'm sorry," said Lucy. The noise from the crowds faded as Dan smiled at her.

"Thank you," he said.

"No. Thank you," said Lucy. "Thank you for making me listen. I want to come next time... to the counselling." Lucy hesitated. "If you still want me to?"

Dan smiled. "Yeah," he said. "I do."

Being trans

Several months ago, a young person I know told me that he was trans. I wanted to understand what he was going through as much as possible, and I was referred to Mermaids UK for further information. What I found were brave and inspiring stories about what it means to be a young trans person in the UK today.

And this got me thinking. What is the best thing about being trans? Where do young trans people get help and support? And what happens if the people they love the most don't support them?

We often assume that it will be the older generations who will struggle with the idea of transitioning, but I quickly learned that this isn't always the case. This is where the idea for Dan and Lucy came from.

I began by looking at websites, reading books, watching some excellent documentaries and, most importantly, talking to members of the trans community. I will be forever grateful to them for the help and advice they gave me when writing this book.

Dan is a fictional character, but so many elements of his story are based on testimonials I read, or on experiences shared with me by trans teenagers and young adults.

Dan is a trans teenager who wants to begin hormone therapy. But not every trans teenager wants hormone therapy, or hormone blockers or gender affirming surgery. Your gender is exactly that: YOURS. You don't need to hit some hidden criteria to be able to identify as trans.

If you are interested in finding out more, or if you are affected by the issues in this story, then you might find the following websites useful:

www.stonewall.org.uk

www.mermaidsuk.org.uk

www.theproudtrust.org

www.akt.org.uk

ABOUT THE AUTHOR

Donna David is a former milkman's assistant, sports coach, ketchup packer and fairground operative.

She lives with her husband and three children in Hampshire but, as part of a military family, they have lived all over the UK.

Now retired from the worlds of milk and ketchup, when Donna's not writing, she works as an English Coach in the local secondary school. Donna loves to read, run and play netball. Not all at once though. Not after last time!

Acknowledgement from the Publisher

Thanks to Alex and Beth at Inclusive Minds (a brilliant team of consultants championing inclusion and diversity) for introducing us to Jo Ross-Barrett through their Young Ambassadors for Inclusion project.

We consulted Jo on the sensitive subject matter in this story, to ensure that it was both authentic and responsible. We are very pleased with the result, and hope you are too.

Jo Ross-Barrett is a non-binary writer and editor with a passion for championing inclusivity. They studied English Language and Literature at the University of Edinburgh and Publishing at Edinburgh Napier University, where they wrote their dissertation on interactive narratives. Since then, their writing has been published by Monstrous Regiment as part of an anthology about bisexuality and related identities.